NO MORE MONSTERS UNDER YOUR BED!

Jordan Chouteau   Illustrated by Anat Even Or

JIMMY PATTERSON BOOKS
LITTLE, BROWN AND COMPANY
NEW YORK BOSTON LONDON

To all my silly monsters: Tom, Brewer, and Wylie. –J. C.

To Alwyn, Gwilym, and Nala. –A. E. O.

Copyright © 2019 by Jordan Chouteau

Illustrations by Anat Even Or

JIMMY Patterson Books / Little, Brown and Company

Hachette Book Group

1290 Avenue of the Americas, New York, NY 10104

JimmyPatterson.org

First Edition: July 2019

JIMMY Patterson Books is an imprint of Little, Brown and Company, a division of Hachette Book Group, Inc. The Little, Brown name and logo are trademarks of Hachette Book Group, Inc. The JIMMY Patterson Books® name and logo are trademarks of JBP Business, LLC.

The publisher is not responsible for websites (or their content) that are not owned by the publisher.

The Hachette Speakers Bureau provides a wide range of authors for speaking events. To find out more, go to hachettespeakersbureau.com or call (866) 376-6591.

ISBN 978-0-316-45388-2

LCCN 2018952839

10 9 8 7 6 5 4 3 2 1

IM

Printed in China

There once was a boy with a monster problem.

Every night, as the monsters
waited for the boy to go to bed,

they hid in his closet,

under his bed,

inside the hamper, and beneath his rug.

One even squeezed into the fishbowl!

And every night, they flicked the lights

on and **off,**

made

BIG *noisy*

toots

and nibbled

at his **toes.**

The boy was worried that if he fell asleep,
the monsters would do horrible things to him.
So he stayed awake all night.

He was afraid of monsters with zillions of eyes watching him,

monsters with zillions of hands grabbing him,

and monsters with cavity-filled teeth gobbling him up
like a bowl of ice cream.

He was afraid of big, hairy monsters, both blond and brunette.

Headless monsters terrified him, too.
Even though they didn't have eyes to see him with.

He was afraid of one-eyed monsters with pigtails, dressed in tutus...

three-headed monsters with curly horns and sticky claws...

and monsters that looked like his grandpa—
they wore socks with sandals like he did, too.

He was afraid of spiky monsters covered in boo-boos,

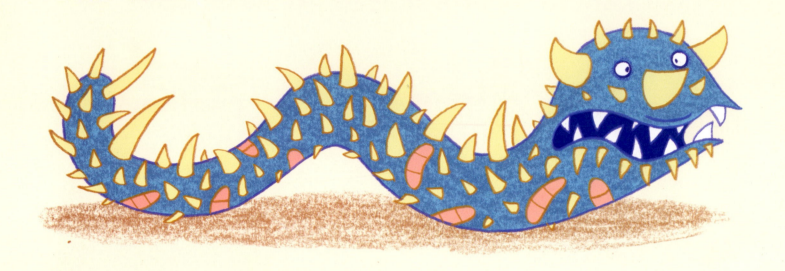

mama monsters, papa monsters, even itty-bitty baby monsters.

They were all so scary,
the boy couldn't get even a wink of sleep.

After many sleepless nights, the boy's parents brought him a special gift—a magic monster patch to put on his pajamas.

The patch had the

Power

to make him

invisible

to all

monsters.

But, they told him, he had to be brave
and believe in the patch for its magic to work.

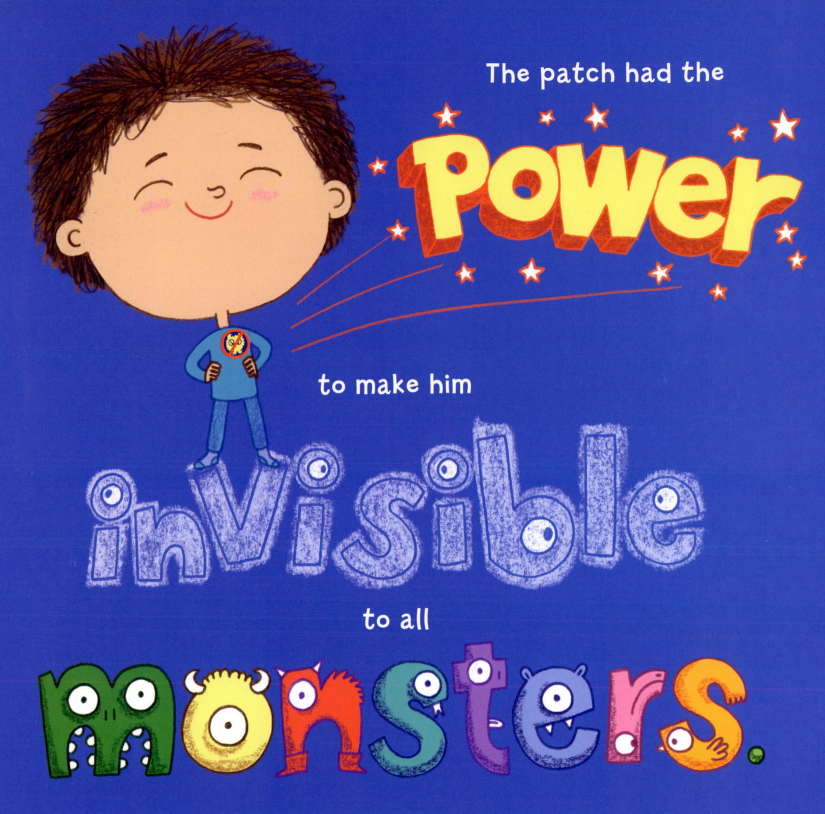

Determined to conquer his monster fears,
the boy stood tall and gathered up all the courage he had.
And then, when he pressed the patch...

...the monsters could no longer see him!

And since they couldn't see him,
they couldn't scare him either.

The boy had been scared of monsters for so long,
he had forgotten what it felt like to not be afraid.

And now that he had the magic monster patch,
he knew he'd never be afraid of monsters again.

He finally felt safe and secure in his bed...
and was able to get some much-needed sleep.

After a few nights, the monsters grew bored
of not having anyone to scare,

so they left the boy's house to find
another kid to poke, bug, and bother.

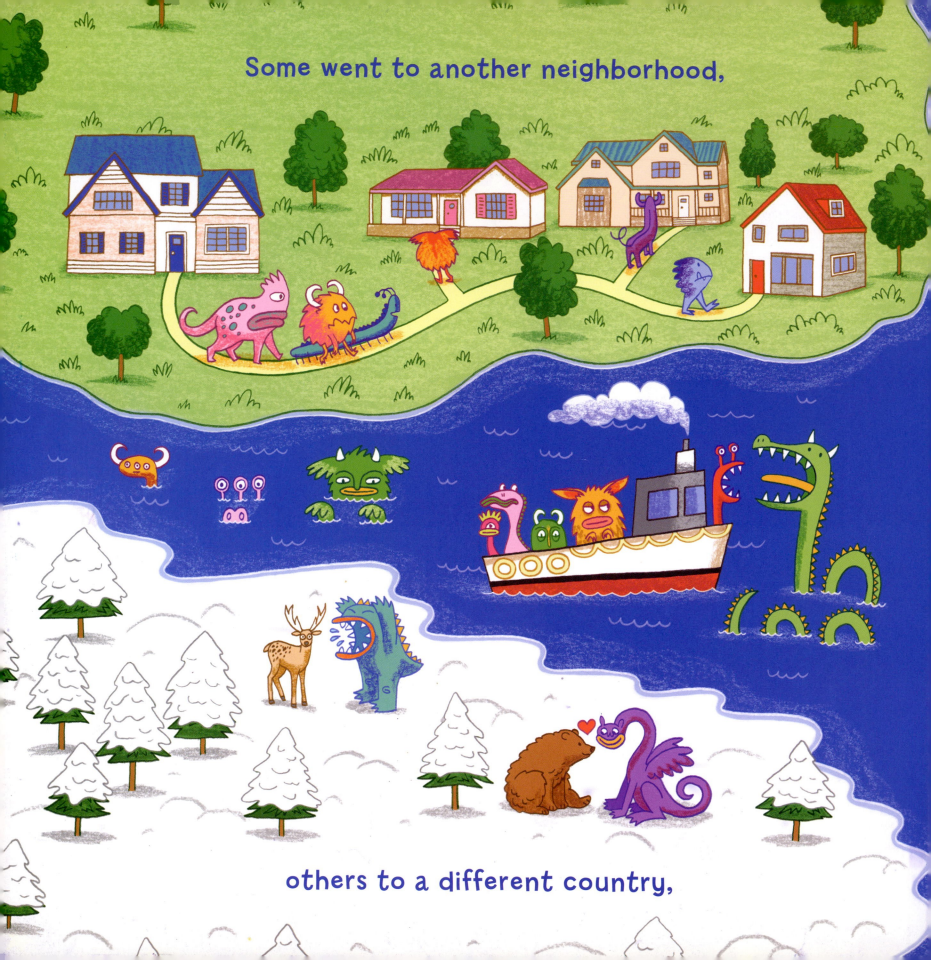

Some went to another neighborhood,

others to a different country,

and some even went to the moon!

Now that the boy wasn't afraid of monsters anymore, he wanted to share the patch to help others overcome the same fear.

So he gave the patch to a friend with a monster-filled bedroom.

She used the patch every night until her monsters finally left.

Then she decided to share the patch with another friend.

They kept sharing and sharing and . . .

Now **you** have the magic monster patch.
It's your turn to get rid of your monsters!

Press the magic patch on your pajamas.

Wow!!!

Now you're

invisible

to all

monsters.

Just remember—after your monsters are all gone,
be sure to pass the patch along so you can help a friend
conquer their fears, too.

The end of this book. And monsters.

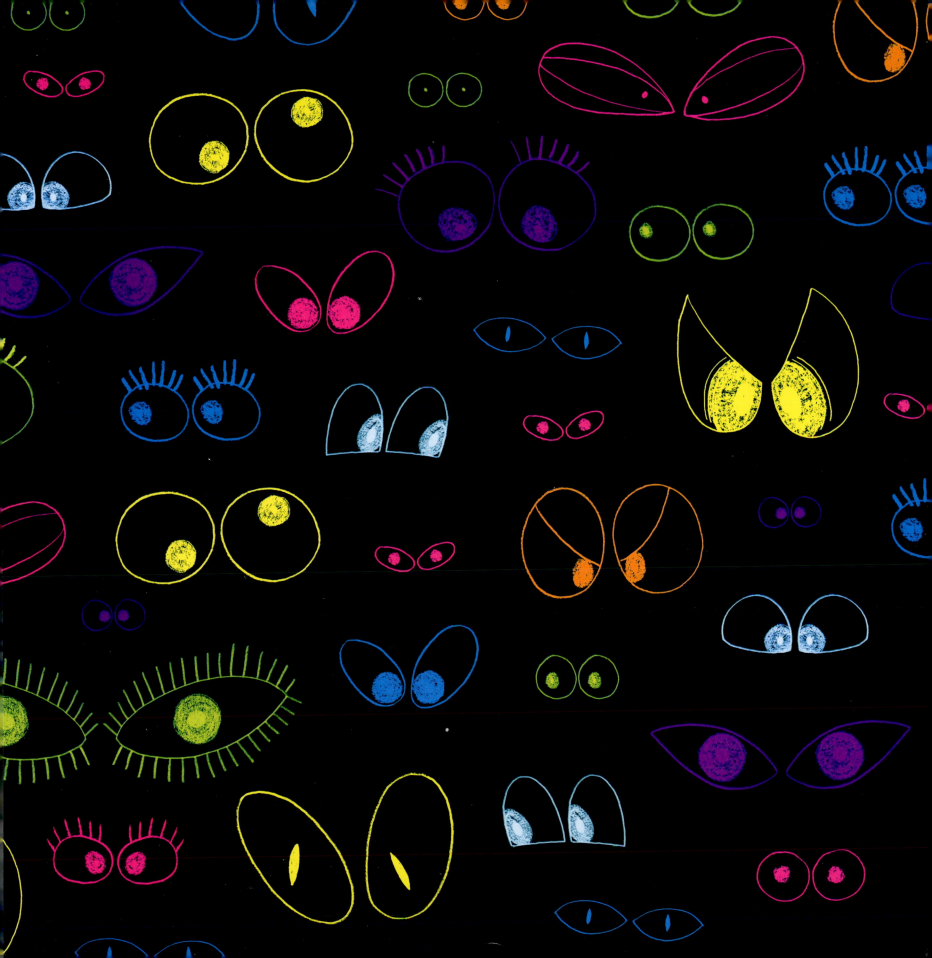